A Birthday for Cow!

JAN THOMAS

Harcourt, Inc.

Orlando Austin New York San Diego London

Printed in China

Toot!

Today is Cow's birthday...

Pig and Mouse are going to make Cow the best birthday cake EVER!

CAKE?!

They put flour and sugar and eggs in a big bowl.

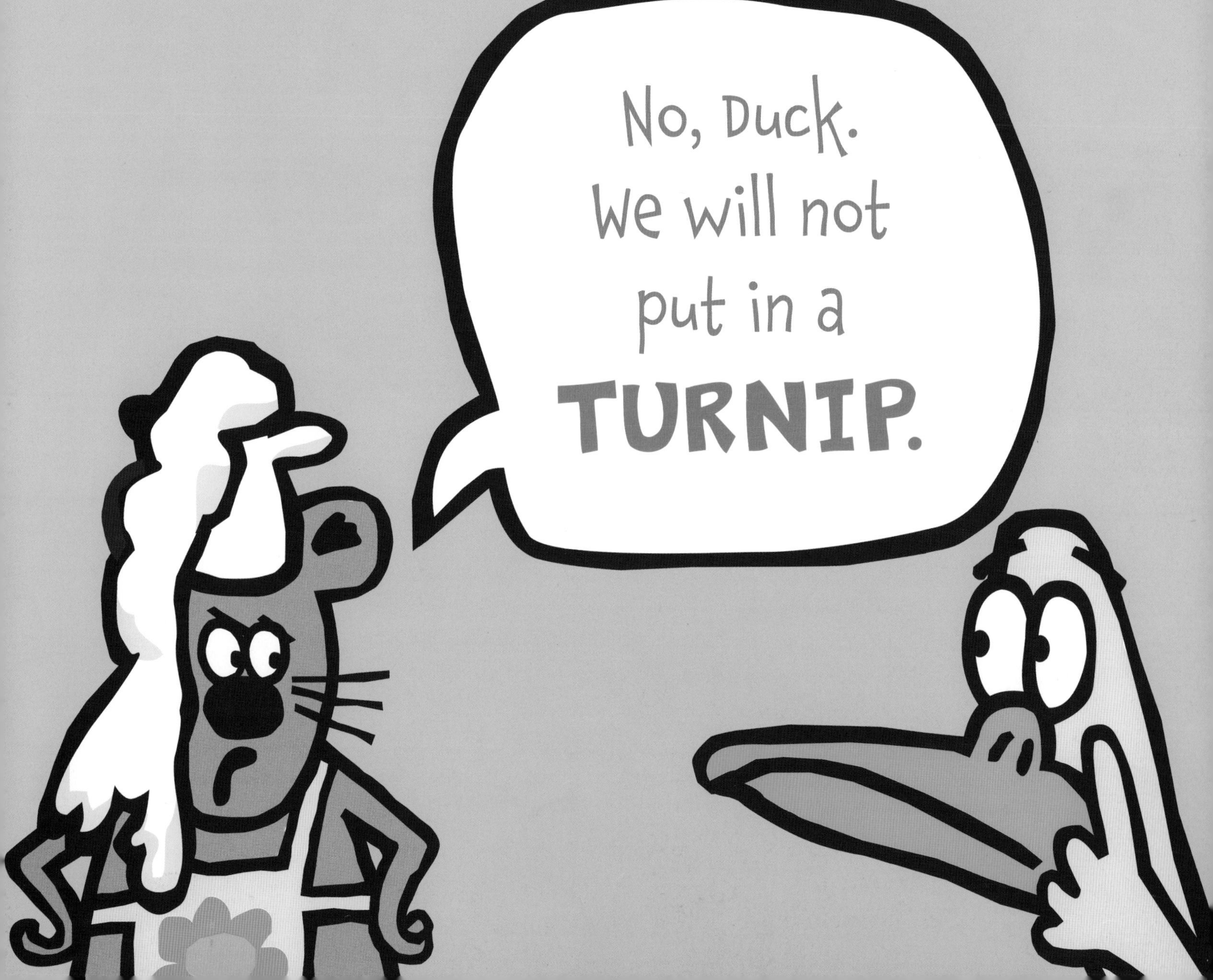
No, Duck. We will not put in a TURNIP.

Next, they mix
it all together
with...

Then they put it
in the oven.

Can a
TURNIP
go in, TOO?

And they ice and decorate the cake, and on top they put...

I know!

Is that what I think it is? Oh boy, this is the best birthday EVER...

Burp!

www.hmhco.com

Library of Congress Cataloging-in-Publication Data
Thomas, Jan, 1958—
A birthday for Cow!/Jan Thomas.
p. cm.
Summary: Despite the objections of Pig and Mouse, Duck insists on adding a special ingredient to the cake they are making to celebrate Cow's birthday.
[1. Cake—Fiction. 2. Birthdays—Fiction. 3. Friendship—Fiction.
4. Animals—Fiction.] I. Title.
PZ7.T36694Bir 2008
[E]—dc22   2007014133
ISBN 978-0-15-206072-5

SCP 8 7 6
4500593408

The display type was set in Eatwell Chubby.
The text type was set in Eatwell Chubby and Chaloops.
Color separations by Colourscan Co. Pte. Ltd., Singapore
Printed and bound by RR Donnelley, China
Production supervision by Christine Witnik
Designed by Michele Wetherbee and Brad Barrett

Sometimes I brush my teeth using a turnip.